The
Three
Armadillies
Tuff

To my grandmother, Florence Rogers,
who knew how to shake her shell on the dance floor—
and to my girls'-night-out friend, Tracy.

A special thanks to Wendy McAdow for her keen eye.
—J. M. H.

To my parents
—S. G. B

Published by
PEACHTREE PUBLISHERS, LTD.
1700 Chattahoochee Avenue
Atlanta, Georgia 30318-2112

www.peachtree-online.com

Text © 2002 by Jackie Mims Hopkins
Illustrations © 2002 by S. G. Brooks

Manufactured in China

Book design by Loraine M. Balcsik
Composition by Melanie M. McMahon
Text typeset in Novarese Book by Fontographer and titles set in Hotsy Totsy by Adobe Systems
Illustrations created in acrylic, gouache, colored pencil, and ink on Bristol paper

10 9 8 7 6 5 4 3 2 1
First Edition

Library of Congress Cataloging-in-Publication Data

Hopkins, Jackie.
    Three Armadillies Tuff / written by Jackie Hopkins ; illustrated by S. G. Brooks.-- 1st ed.
        p. cm.
Summary: In this humorous version of "Three Billy Goats Gruff," three armadillo sisters encounter a strange
creature in a culvert when they try to go dancing.
    ISBN 1-56145-258-0
    PZ8.H7785 Th 2002
    [398.2]--dc21   2001005567

The Three Armadillies Tuff

Jackie Mims Hopkins

Illustrated by

S. G. Brooks

Ω

PEACHTREE
ATLANTA

Once there were three armadillo sisters by the name of Tuff. The smallest was Lilly, a humdinger of a gal who really knew how to shake her shell on the dance floor. The middle sister was Jilly, the fashion queen of the family. The biggest sister was Dilly, who was crazy about chowin' down. My, my, how those three armadillies loved to have a good time!

In fact, it was their quest for fun and adventure that got them in trouble one warm summer evening.

"Let's go to that new dance hall on the other side of the highway," suggested Lilly. "I have a hankerin' to learn some new steps and kick up my claws."

"But if we run across the highway, I might chip my nails!" complained Jilly, inspecting a freshly painted claw.

"Or get squashed by an eighteen-wheeler," Dilly added.

"Oh, don't be such soft-shelled ninnies!" Lilly scoffed. "We can cut through the big drainpipe that runs under the road."

The sisters all agreed that this was a fine idea, so they waddled off toward the highway.

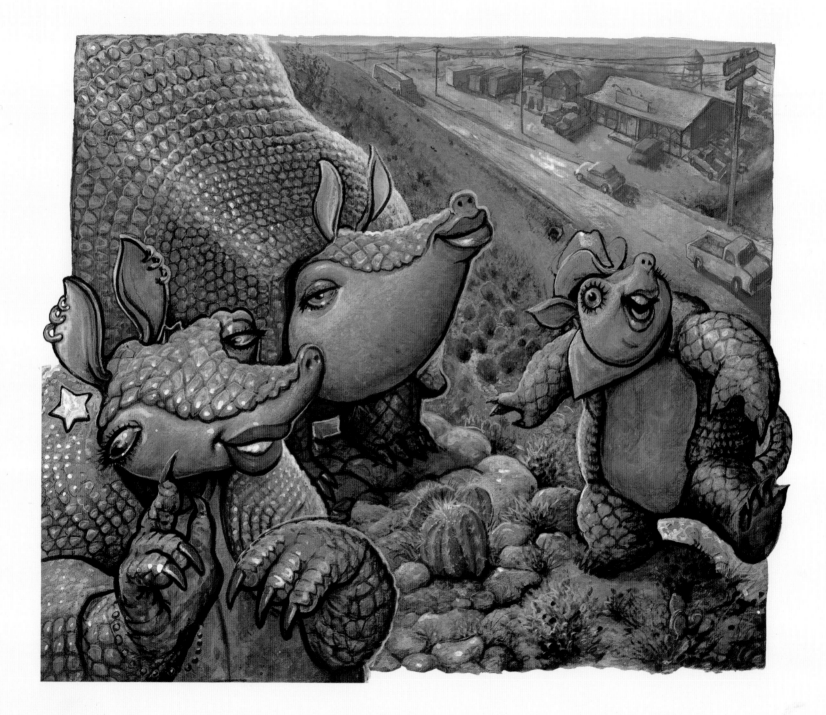

By and by, the sisters arrived at the culvert and peered into the long, dark pipe.

"I'll go first," Lilly volunteered bravely.

Scritch, scratch, scritch, scratch, Lilly sashayed her way along.

"Who's that scritch, scratchin' through my tunnel?" growled a voice.

"It's just me, Lilly Armadilly Tuff," the smallest sister replied.

"Come closer," snarled the voice.

As Lilly stepped forward, she saw a spindly legged coyote with glowing eyes, glaring at her hungrily.

"Whooee!" exclaimed Lilly, jumping back. She tried to ignore the coyote's pointy fangs. "From the looks of those scrawny legs, I'd say you need a workout."

"What I need," panted the coyote, "is a nice hot bowl of armadilly chili."

Lilly thought fast. "My bigger sister is right behind me. She'd make a much better chili than I would," she suggested.

The scraggly coyote scratched behind an ear for a moment. "Go on, then," she barked finally. "Git!"

Lilly scurried away before the coyote could change her mind.

Soon after, the second sister waddled into the tunnel. She was very careful not to let the cobwebs catch in her jewelry.

Scritch, scratch, scritch, scratch, Jilly jangled her way along.

"Who's that scritch, scratchin' through my tunnel?" growled the coyote.

"It's just me, Jilly Armadilly Tuff," the middle sister replied.

"Come closer," the coyote demanded.

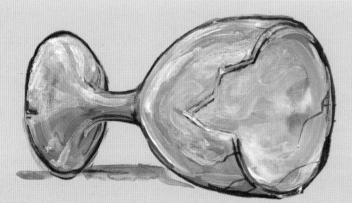

As Jilly stepped forward, she saw drool dripping off the coyote's long tongue and onto the critter's grungy coat.

"Yikes!" yipped Jilly. "That slobbery mouth of yours sure needs sprucin' up. And from the looks of your mangy old fur, I'd say you need a good soak in the tub."

"What I need," snapped the coyote, looking Jilly up and down, "is a nice hot bowl of armadilly chili and some fancy armadillo skin boots."

"Whoa! Hold on, fleabag," replied Jilly, holding up a claw. "In that case, you'll be wantin' my big—and I do mean BIG—sister Dilly. She's on her way here right now. Dilly will not only fill you up and make you a fine pair of boots, but she might even fetch you a handbag, too!"

"A handbag?" The scraggly coyote's beady eyes grew larger and she stopped drooling for a moment. Then she licked her chops and barked, "Go on, then! Git!"

Jilly skittered out of that tunnel lickety-split.

A few minutes later, the third sister squeezed into the tunnel.

Scritch, scratch, scritch, scratch, Dilly lumbered her way along.

"Who's that scritch, scratchin' through my tunnel?" howled the coyote.

"It's just me, Dilly Armadilly Tuff," the biggest sister replied. "I'm trying to catch up with my sisters."

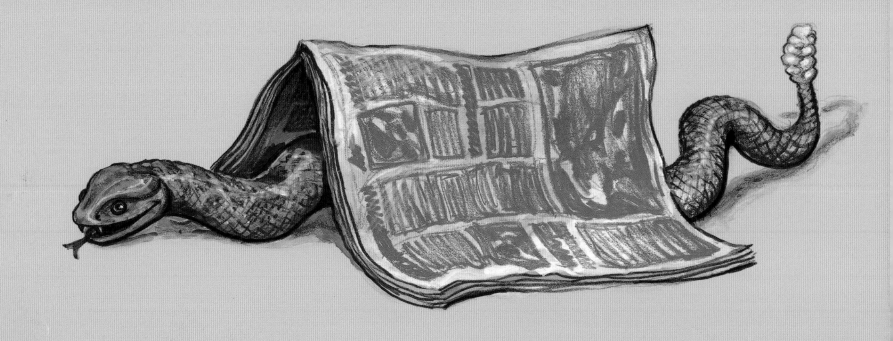

"Well, your sisters aren't here," snarled the coyote. "But they promised you would make me a fine meal, some boots, and a handbag."

"Who, *me*?" Dilly said. "Why, that's downright ridiculous! I'm no good at cookin' or sewin'. But I know where we can find ourselves somethin' good to eat and have some fun."

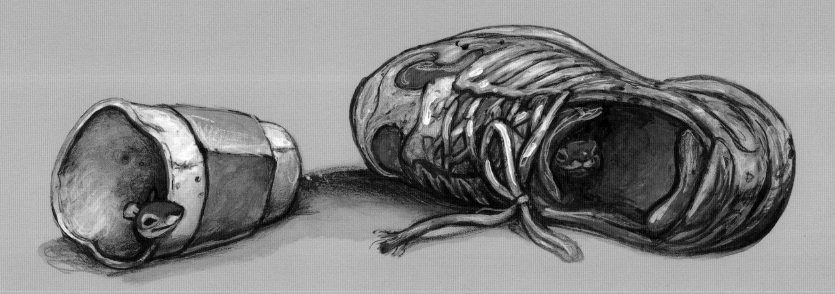

With a growl, the coyote stepped out of the shadows, and Dilly got a good, long look at her.

"Mercy!" Dilly yelped. "I mean, why, you poor thing. How long has it been since you've had a girls' night out?"

"A what?" asked the coyote, frowning.

"You know, a night out on the town," Dilly explained. "With friends."

The coyote sniffed. "I've always been a loner," she said sadly. "I've never had any friends."

"Well, bless your little ol' heart," Dilly cried. "We can fix that! Come on, let's go find my sisters."

When Lilly and Jilly heard the coyote's sad story, the three sisters treated the pitiful critter (whose name, by the way, was Tallula) to a fluff-and-puff makeover and a fine meal at the trash cans behind the Chomp and Stomp.

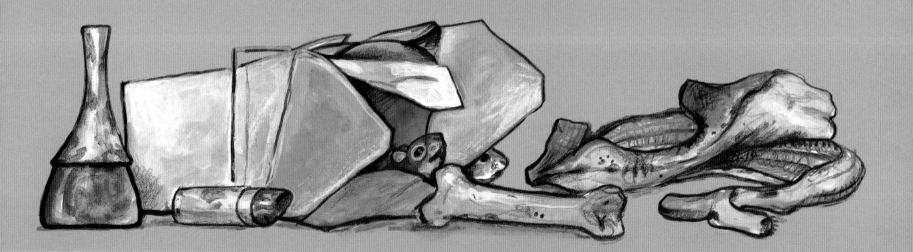

Before long, Tallula was lookin' fine in
her new hair bow, FAKE leather boots, and
a matching handbag. Then it was time to
hit the dance floor, where Lilly taught them
all how to do the Armadilly Shuffle.

So, if you ever hear critters digging through garbage cans or a coyote howling, don't fret. It's just Tallula and the Armadilly Tuff sisters having a rip-roaring good time!